SCOOBY-DOO!
Mystery #2

The Frozen Giant

Howard

illustrated by
Duendes del Sur

SCHOLASTIC INC.
New York   Toronto   London   Auckland
Sydney   Mexico City   New Delhi   Hong Kong

ISBN 978-0-545-38677-7

12 11 10 9 8 7 6 5 4 3   12 13 14 15 16 17/0

Designed by Henry Ng

Printed in the U.S.A.   40

First printing, February 2012

CHAPTER

The Mystery Machine slid around a corner on the icy road. "I feel like I'm in a sled!" Shaggy cried, lifting his hands in the air. "Wheeee!"

"Reah!" Scooby barked. "Reeeeee!"

Fred stayed focused on the road in front of

them. "This fresh snow sure does make the road slippery. But we should be there soon."

Daphne peered out of the van's window. She was admiring the snow-capped hills that surrounded them. "This fluffy snow is going to make for some great snowshoeing and sledding this weekend. It's a winter wonderland," she said.

"I'm looking forward to seeing the ice sculptures," Velma put in. She glanced up from the booklet she'd been reading. "According to this, some ice artists have been working on houses that are made out of ice and snow. It takes them several weeks to carve them. People can even sleep in them after they're finished. It's a real engineering feat."

"*My* feet aren't going anywhere near a house made out of ice," Shaggy said, shivering. "But do you think any of the houses might be made out of ice *cream*?" He licked his lips. "I'd sign up to sleep in that!"

The kids from Mystery, Inc. were taking a weekend vacation in a small town called Giant's Ridge. It was supposed to be perfect for cross-country skiing, winter hiking, ice-cave exploring, and snowshoeing. A new developer was throwing a huge Ice Carnival to celebrate the winter season and welcome people to the town.

"We're almost there," Fred said, turning onto a narrow drive. He peered at the snowy road ahead. "Look, gang. That must be the hill they call Giant's Ridge. The town is named after it." He pointed to a long, rocky ridge that seemed to stretch for miles in front of them. The top of the hill was hidden by swirling snow and fog.

"Jeepers. I sure hope the Ice Carnival is being held at the bottom of that hill," Daphne said. "It looks awfully cold up at the top."

"Not to mention the sleeping giant Velma was telling us about," Shaggy said. "I think I'd rather *eat* the food at the Ice Carnival than get *eaten* at the Ice Carnival, if you know what I mean. Like, if that giant's really been sleeping for a thousand years, he's going to be pretty hungry when he wakes up!"

"Ree-hee-hee," Scooby giggled.

"The giant's not real, Shaggy," Velma said. "It's just part of the legend. Some people think the hills around the town look like a sleeping giant, so they named it Giant's Ridge."

"It's obviously just a story," Daphne added.

"Legend, schmegend. I'm not taking any chances," Shaggy said.

"Reah. Ro riants!" Scooby agreed.

The Mystery Machine cruised to the end of the road. Fred parked it next to a bunch of other cars.

The gang followed a short trail through the woods. The path was lit with cheerful, twinkling lights, and lined with signs that said: WELCOME TO GIANT'S RIDGE! ICE CARNIVAL THIS WAY! and OUR TOWN WELCOMES YOU BACK! and HOMEMADE MAPLE ICE CREAM—SHARE OUR SECRET RECIPE!

"Homemade maple ice cream?" Shaggy read the sign hungrily. "Like, you don't have to tell me twice! I'm not so sure about sharing, though."

Scooby sniffed at an ice cream cone that had been carved out of ice. He licked it, then took a timid bite. "Rummy," he said, crunching his teeth to break up the ice.

"Like, Scoob?" Shaggy said, holding up the last bits of crumbled ice. "I think that was just a decoration."

"Rit rasted rood!" Scooby said.

As the gang turned a corner, they saw someone standing in front of one of the welcome signs. It was a woman wearing snowshoes. She had a compass and tools hanging from her belt. When they got closer, they noticed that she was spray-painting a big, glittering red X over one of the welcome signs.

"Hey! What are you doing?" Velma asked.

The woman turned around, startled. Then she returned to what she'd been doing. "People *aren't* welcome," she said angrily. "These signs make it seem like we're happy to have people tromping through our forest and hills. But I'm not! I wish all these visitors would just turn around and go home. Leave Giant's Ridge alone!"

Velma and Fred glanced at each other.

"You're not looking forward to the Ice Carnival?" Daphne asked politely.

"No!" the woman snapped. "How do you think the animals feel about all these people invading their forest, tracking through their land? Do you think the bears are happy people are wandering around while they try to hibernate?"

"Rares?" Scooby said, shuddering. "Rhut rares?"

"I'm Lynn Johnson, and I study the animals in the forest around Giant's Ridge," the woman explained. "We've lived together in peace for the past twenty years. Now people are going to tromp around and push the animals out—and then where will we go?"

No one knew what to say. But that was okay, because Lynn Johnson didn't wait for them to answer. She took one last look at the gang, then stormed off into the woods.

"I guess not everyone is excited about the Ice Carnival," Velma observed. "She sure wasn't very friendly."

Suddenly, the path ended and the gang found themselves at one end of Main Street in Giant's Ridge. A small, peaceful town sprawled in front of them. Little shops and inns lined the street. Food vendors were perched on every corner. Lights twinkled from tree branches, and welcome banners hung everywhere.

"It *is* a winter wonderland," Daphne said happily. "Lynn Johnson might not be excited about the carnival, but I just know this is going to be groovy."

Suddenly, Velma pointed. "Guys! Look!"

There, up on the top of the ridge, was a huge, white creature. But in an instant, before anyone could get a good look at it, the beast disappeared behind the hill.

CHAPTER 2

"**Z**oinks!" Shaggy cried, hiding behind Scooby-Doo.

"Well, that was strange," Fred said.

"What was it?" Daphne asked.

"It must have just been the snow," Velma said,

shaking her head. "The way the snow is swirling and blowing, it almost looked like there was a creature up on the ridge."

"Reature?" Scooby said.

"I'm sure it was nothing," Fred reassured them. "Just a trick of the wind."

As the gang stood there, staring up into the snowy hills, a woman in a thick snowsuit and big, furry boots bounded up to them. "Enjoying the snowfall, are you?" She shook paws with Scooby. "Welcome! I'm Norah Malone, the developer of this glorious winter village. I hope you're looking forward to the Ice Carnival!"

"Hello, Ms. Malone," Fred said. He shook her hand. "I'm Fred, and this is Daphne, Velma, Shaggy, and Scooby-Doo."

"Scooby who?" Ms. Malone said with a laugh. "It's a pleasure to meet you all. Please, call me

9

Norah." She winked at them. "We're all friends here in Giant's Ridge."

"That's right!" A loud, shrill voice boomed out from behind them. "We're all friends around here."

Shaggy and Scooby turned. They saw a tall woman wearing a sleek black overcoat. The woman narrowed her eyes at Norah and gave her a cold smile. "Norah, I hope we will *still* be friends after everyone realizes that this sad little village is nothing compared to Hooperman's Resort!" She gave the gang a thumbs-up, then grabbed a bag of donuts off a nearby food stand.

"Hooperman's Resort?" Shaggy asked.

"My resort is the best place on earth," the woman said. "At Hooperman's, you don't have to worry about frozen giants."

As the woman laughed and walked away, Norah rolled her eyes. "Don't mind Isabella," she said. "She owns Hooperman's Resort, which is just a few miles away. She's upset that we're opening Giant's Ridge for business. They haven't had much competition over at Hooperman's since they opened twenty years ago. I think she's a little nervous that some of her customers are going to start coming here for winter getaways, instead of to her resort."

"This is a beautiful town," Daphne observed. "I can see why Isabella Hooperman would be nervous. Giant's Ridge looks like a wonderful winter vacation spot."

Norah smiled. "There's plenty of business for all of us. In fact, years ago, Giant's Ridge was an incredibly popular tourist spot. That's why I decided to revive the town. You see, I was born here, and I was always disappointed that Giant's Ridge turned into something of a ghost town. And all because of something so silly. . . ." She stopped talking and glanced up into the hills.

"Why did Giant's Ridge close down, Norah?" Velma asked. "Why did people move away?"

"Right after Hooperman's Resort opened for business, someone started a terrible rumor that scared everyone away. The visitors *and* the people who lived here year-round all left." Norah frowned. "Have you heard the legend of our sleeping giant?" she asked.

"Only what we read in this booklet," Velma said. "Isn't that just an old story?"

"Yes," Norah said. "There's an old legend that

says a thousand-year-old giant is sleeping inside the ice caves that are hidden under the hills that surround the town. They say he's frozen under that ridge." She glanced up into the hills, and then lowered her voice. "About twenty years ago, someone started telling people that the giant had woken up and was going to come down the hill and take over the town. That was enough to scare everyone away."

"Like, did it ever happen?" Shaggy asked. His voice was shaking.

"Of course not," Norah said. She smiled warmly at the gang. "It's just a silly story. You can all just relax and enjoy yourselves." She turned around and gestured down Main Street. "If you walk this way, you'll end up at our town square. There you can watch the ice artists working on their carvings. They've been working for several weeks to build and carve their designs for beautiful ice houses. Tomorrow we'll have a prize ceremony to choose the best house. The winner will be awarded fifty thousand dollars."

"Like, that's a lot of cash," Shaggy said, his eyes wide. "Is it too late for me to build a house out of ice?"

Norah laughed. "Yes, I'm afraid so. The ice artists have come from all around the world to compete. It's going to be very difficult to choose a winner! They're all incredibly talented . . . and very competitive with one another. The designs are all unique and creative." She put her finger up in the air, as if she'd just remembered something. "But, Shaggy, it's not too late for you to enter the ice-cream eating contest. The winner of that contest will get a year's supply of maple ice cream as a prize. Would that be okay?"

"Like, that sounds even better to me!" Shaggy cried. "Scoob, old pal, I hope you're hungry!" He looked around and realized Scooby was no longer next to him. "Scooby?!"

"Rhut?" Scooby was standing at a nearby food cart, shoveling tacos into his mouth. "Ri'm racticing!"

CHAPTER 3

T he gang wandered toward the town's square, passing crowds of cheerful visitors. Ice houses lined the outer edge of the square. Some were more than two stories tall!

Snow had finally stopped falling, and the sun

was peeking through the clouds. The light glinted off the ice carvings as people milled around the town square, admiring the artists' work.

"Yoo-hoo! Scooby-Doo!" Shaggy called. Scooby looked around the mounds of ice and snow, trying to find his friend. Snowplows had piled snow in large heaps throughout the square. The snow piles were being carved into beautiful, icy art.

"Raggy?" Scooby called. He peeked under carved ice fish and around an ice shark.

"Like, over here!" Shaggy waved out a round window in one of the ice structures. It was a house that had been built to look like a pirate ship. There was even a real fishing net hanging out over the edge of the boat. Scooby poked his head around the net. "Ahoy, Scoob, ye scurvy dog!"

Scooby chuckled, then slipped a pirate hat made of ice onto his head. "Ralk the rank, Raggy!" He pointed at an icy shelf that was jutting out from the side of the ice boat.

"Don't you dare," growled a menacing voice. "I want you out of my boat."

Scooby and Shaggy poked their heads around the side of the boat. One of the ice artists was watching them carefully. He was holding a sharp carving tool in one hand.

"Like, ahoy," Shaggy said, stepping carefully out of the icy ship. "Nice boat, sir. It looks like you're frozen in. Not sailing far today, huh?" Shaggy saluted the man, who frowned at them.

"You need to watch your step," the man said angrily. "I have to keep an eye on people around here." He looked around suspiciously. "This is a big prize, and I don't want anyone ruining my work before I win."

"We understand," Fred said, joining them. "This ship doesn't look like it would have been easy to carve out of ice. How long have you been working on it?"

The man sighed. "I've spent the last three weeks here, building this ship. All I've got left to paint is the outside. Gotta make her shine like the South Seas!" He held up a can of spray paint. "I'm going to make the flag black, the ship's sides will sparkle with a glittering red paint, and the snow around the ship is going to be painted blue, like the ocean."

"That sounds beautiful," Daphne said.

"It better be enough to win," the man said. "I'm Soren Gray, the best ice carver in the world." He looked around at the other ice carvers. They were all hard at work, minding their own business and putting the finishing touches on their art. "If you'll excuse me, I need to grab another can of paint from my supplies. Keep an eye on the other carvers for me—I don't trust anyone around here!"

The gang watched as Soren marched away from the town's square. "I guess the competition is really heating up," Velma said.

"Like, I hope it doesn't heat up enough to melt all the ice houses," Shaggy laughed. "Get it? Heat up?"

Velma rolled her eyes. "Let's take a look around at the other artists' work. Scooby, Shaggy, try not to touch anything!"

The gang wandered through the square,

admiring the rest of the ice carvings. The other artists seemed to be having much more fun than Soren Gray. Some carvers were inviting people into their ice houses to see their work. One artist was even letting a little girl help paint with a shiny green wax.

Daphne stopped to admire the woman's work. She had built a huge ice castle, complete with sparkling turrets and a moat. The artist was finishing an ice dragon that was peeking out of the icy water. "This ice castle is really groovy," Daphne exclaimed.

"Thanks," the artist responded. "I'm Sabrina, and this is my first big ice carving competition. I'm really nervous!"

"You don't need to be nervous," Fred said. "This castle is definitely the best ice sculpture here. All the other artists here should be worried about competing against *you*!"

Sabrina smiled. "Thanks a lot. I better get back to work, though. I still have a lot to do before the judging tomorrow."

"And I still have a lot of practicing to do before the ice-cream eating contest tomorrow!" Shaggy said. "Like, Scoob, let's head over there and check out the food carts."

Scooby and Shaggy were drawn toward the smell of spun sugar and fresh maple cakes. The crowd was thick in the town's square, and people seemed to be having a great time.

Suddenly, there was a loud shriek. Someone shouted, "It's the frozen giant! Everyone . . . run!"

People looked around and screamed, then fled, ducking under ice sculptures and diving behind park benches.

Scooby and Shaggy hid inside a hot dog cart, watching as a huge, icy beast roared through the town. It was pale as the snow, with pointy ears like a wolf's and an angry-looking expression on its face.

As the beast tore through the town square, it threw something at the ice carvings that melted them on contact. The creature rose up, lifting its arms in the air, and towered over the crowd. Icicles hung from its frozen arms, and water dripped from its mouth as it roared.

The beast ran toward the beautiful ice castle and grabbed Sabrina. "Help!" she screamed. "Put me down!" But the beast charged on, carrying Sabrina over its frozen shoulder. Sabrina kicked and shouted, hitting the creature's shoulders and back.

But it was no use. The creature was too strong for her. It stomped through town, destroying everything in its wake!

CHAPTER 4

T he beast stormed down Main Street in Giant's Ridge before finally disappearing into the woods. Everyone could hear Sabrina screaming as the giant disappeared into the trees.

Slowly, people started to emerge from under ice

sculptures and from inside the buildings they'd been hiding in.

Scooby and Shaggy peeked out from under a mound of hot dog buns. They had piled them up to look like an igloo. "Like, was that what I think it was?" Shaggy asked.

"Rice reast!" Scooby said.

"That was no ice beast," someone shouted. "That was the frozen giant! It's true—the frozen giant is real. We need to get out of here!"

"That's right," Isabella Hooperman yelled from the edge of the square. "Everyone is welcome over at Hooperman's Resort. Giant's Ridge just isn't safe. It never was. We'll be serving hot chocolate and cookies in our lodge for anyone who would like to join us. You're all welcome. Get out of here before it's too late!"

People started to flow down Giant's Ridge's Main Street, heading for the safety of their cars and Hooperman's Resort.

Norah Malone waved her arms in the air. "Wait! Everyone! Please don't go." She looked around sadly.

Even the artists were packing up their stuff and preparing to leave. Norah tried to stop them. "You can't leave! The ice-house judging is tomorrow. We'll be choosing a winner! Don't you want to finish your designs so you have a chance to win the prize?"

"It's not worth the money," one of the artists said. "That horrible giant kidnapped Sabrina! Then it melted the front door of my ice house. What is that horrible thing going to do next? I'm getting out of here before it's too late!"

Several other artists nodded. They packed their tools, leaving their ice houses unfinished. The rest of the crowd had already thinned, and there were only a few people left in the town's square with Scooby and the gang.

Suddenly, the sound of laughter rang out from behind Scooby and Shaggy's hot-dog-bun igloo. They turned and saw Lynn Johnson, the woman who had been spray-painting *X*'s on the welcome signs. "I guess my wish came true," she said. "Sorry about your little carnival, kids. But it looks like it's time to go home and leave me and the animals alone."

"Not so fast," Fred said. "Norah, we need to find that giant and rescue Sabrina."

"I know," Norah said. She was very upset. "How are we ever going to find them? The giant could be anywhere."

"Yes," Velma agreed. "But lucky for you, mysteries are our specialty."

"Really?" Norah asked. "You'd be willing to help?"

Fred looked at the others. "Gang, it looks like we've got a mystery on our hands. And we need to work quickly, before someone gets hurt!"

"The first thing we need to do is look for clues," Velma said. She adjusted her glasses, watching as Lynn Johnson snowshoed back into the woods. "We have to figure out where that giant came from, and where it took Sabrina."

"Actually," Shaggy said, "the first thing we need to do is follow Isabella Hooperman over to Hooperman's Resort. Like, didn't you hear her say there would be hot chocolate and cookies in the lodge?"

Scooby nodded. "Rookies!"

"Scooby, Shaggy, the frozen giant kidnapped someone!" Daphne scolded. "And all you can think about is cookies?"

"Like, I was just thinking I don't want to be the giant's next meal," Shaggy said. "He looked awfully hungry."

"Actually," Velma said, "there are some things about that so-called giant that seem awfully suspicious. Take a look at this!"

Everyone hurried over to Velma. She was studying tracks in the snow. "These are the giant's footprints." She pointed. "You can tell from the prints that this giant was just wearing a pair of regular winter boots."

Fred studied another boot track. "Hmm, a giant who lives inside the mountain wouldn't need human boots," he observed.

"That's exactly what I was thinking," Velma said. "I wonder if someone is dressing up like the giant to try to scare us away?"

"Should we follow the tracks through the

woods?" Norah Malone suggested. "Hopefully they'll lead us to Sabrina."

Fred nodded. "That's a great idea. Keep your eye out for clues, gang. We might see something along the way."

Norah led the gang through the frozen woods. They followed the giant's tracks through the snow. "The caves are right up ahead," Norah said, pointing to dark mounds that stuck up out of the ground.

As they walked toward the caves, the giant's tracks became harder to follow. Fresh snow had blown over them, and soon they lost the giant's trail completely. "I think we've hit a dead end, gang," Fred said.

"Hey, look over there!" Daphne called, pointing to something bright glinting in a snowbank.

Scooby slipped his head behind Shaggy's puffy, down jacket to hide. "Riant?" he asked.

"No, Scooby, it's not the giant," Velma said. She shook her head. "It's just red glitter—it looks a little like paint." She bent down to study it more closely. "That's another great clue, Daphne. And look, here's another footprint! The giant must have come this way."

"Listen!" Norah cried out suddenly. "I hear someone calling for help. I wonder if it's Sabrina!"

"We should split up so we can find her faster," Fred suggested. "Daphne, Norah, and I will look inside that cave over there." He pointed to the entrance of an ice cave about fifteen feet in front of them.

"And Scooby, Shaggy, and I will look in here." Velma pointed to the dark, icy mouth of the cave a few feet to their left. It looked cold and scary.

Daphne nodded. "Let's all meet right back here in a few minutes."

Everyone except Scooby and Shaggy started into the caves. "After you, Scooby-Doo," Shaggy said, stepping behind Scooby.

"Ro, rafter rou," Scooby said, prancing through the snow to hide behind Shaggy.

"Oh, come on. I'll go first. This way, guys!" Velma called. She motioned for Scooby and Shaggy to follow her as she strode into the dark cave. Scooby and Shaggy reluctantly followed.

Inside the cave, it took a minute for their eyes to adjust to the darkness. When they finally did, they could see gleaming icicles hanging from the roof of the cave. The ground beneath their feet was slick with ice and snow.

Suddenly, Velma slipped. As she fell, her glasses flew off. "Jinkies! I lost my glasses!" she cried, feeling around on the ground around her. The thick mittens she was wearing didn't help, so she pulled them off. Her hand passed over something hard and rubbery. Then she felt something cold and icy under her bare hand.

"Hey, Velma," Shaggy called from the other side of the cave. "Like, I found your glasses. They slid all the way over here."

Velma stood up . . . and found herself face-to-face with the frozen giant!

"Um, Shaggy? Scooby?" Velma squinted. She was trying to figure out if her eyes were tricking her. "I think I may have found the frozen giant." She reached out a hand to touch the giant's frozen skin. It was icy and a little hairy. Velma pulled her hand back quickly.

"Zoinks!" Shaggy cried, handing Velma her glasses. He grabbed Velma's arm and pulled her along behind him. "Like, run!"

Scooby, Shaggy, and Velma slipped and slid as they ran toward the mouth of the cave and away from the frozen giant. The giant was just a few steps behind them as they jumped and leaped over piles of snow and frozen icicles. It grunted and growled, lifting its arms high in the air.

"Rikes!" Scooby called. "Raggy, relp!"

Shaggy stopped to look back. The giant had caught hold of Scooby's tail and was dragging him back into the cave.

"Scoob! Hold on, buddy!" Shaggy cried as he slipped on the icy cave floor. He jumped out of the way just in time as a long, sharp icicle fell from the roof of the cave.

"We're coming to get you, Scooby," Velma called.

The giant was pulling Scooby farther and farther into the cave. It was almost impossible for Velma and Shaggy to see their friend! They knew they had to move fast or Scooby would become the giant's next prisoner.

Velma and Shaggy followed the giant into the dark tunnels that led deeper into the cave. Finally, they spotted Scooby as the giant tried to round a corner deep inside the cave.

"Grab him, Shaggy!" Velma cried. They reached for Scooby and grabbed his two front paws. They pulled at the front of his body as the giant pulled at the back. Scooby's body stretched between them until, finally, *snap*! The giant lost its grip on Scooby's tail. Velma, Shaggy, and Scooby fell in a heap against the cave wall.

"Like, run!" Shaggy called. "Again!"

This time, Scooby zipped ahead of Shaggy and Velma. The giant roared behind them. With every stomp of the giant's foot, icicles fell from the cave's ceiling and came crashing down around them. Shaggy ducked and leaped. He was just steps behind Scooby.

Finally, they reached the mouth of the cave and escaped into the bright, snowy forest. They ran a long way before slowing down.

"Like, that was close," Shaggy said at last.

"Raggy?" Scooby said, tapping Shaggy on the shoulder.

"Not now, old pal. I need to take a little rest. Rescuing friends from a frozen giant is hard work!"

Scooby pointed behind him. "Raggy, rook!"

Shaggy turned. That's when he realized the giant was still chasing them. It had just barreled out of the mouth of the cave. Now it was running straight toward them.

Even worse, Velma was nowhere to be seen!

CHAPTER 7

Shaggy and Scooby started running again. They flew over snow banks and zipped around trees. Scooby's paws spun and slipped out from under him as he slid over an icy log and fell to the ground. His face landed in the snow. "Rouch,"

Scooby whined. He blew snow out of his nose and mouth.

"Hey, Scoob, watch this," Shaggy said. He hid behind a huge pine tree. As soon as the giant went rushing past, Shaggy pelted the creature with snowballs.

"Ree-hee-hee," Scooby giggled. The giant had to lift its huge arms to protect itself from the snowball attack. But Scooby stopped laughing when Shaggy ran out of snowballs. The giant turned and roared at them again.

Scooby began to run first, with Shaggy close on his heels. They moved as fast as they could in their snow gear, but both of them fell a few times. Once they went sliding down a hill on their backsides. "Reeee!" Scooby cried.

Just when Shaggy and Scooby thought they couldn't run anymore, the giant raised its arms and gave one final growl. Then it turned and charged back through the woods.

"Like, that was close," Shaggy said, panting. He sat on the ground to rest. "This belly is going to need some serious fuel before our next chase." He poked around in his jacket pockets and found a dusty old Scooby Snack. "Like, look at this! It's my lucky day." He tossed the snack up in the air and opened his mouth to catch it.

Scooby reached his tongue out and grabbed the Scooby Snack out of the air before Shaggy could eat it. He chomped happily. "Ranks, Raggy."

"Hey, guys!" Fred called through the trees. "What are you doing way over here? I thought we were all meeting back by the caves."

Shaggy and Scooby stood up and shook the snow off. They tripped over each other as they hustled to get to Fred. Daphne and Norah were right behind him.

"Like, first we found the frozen giant," Shaggy said quickly. He pointed. "In that cave you made us look in, back there."

"Reah," Scooby nodded. He raised up on his back legs and waved his arms around in the air like the giant had done. "Riant . . . *rooooooar!*"

"Then that frozen beast got Scooby-Doo," Shaggy said. "Like, it grabbed him by the tail, and we had to play tug-of-war to get our old buddy back."

Scooby covered his eyes, remembering how scared he'd been when the giant pulled at his tail. He wrapped his tail around his body and hugged it tight. "Rit rot re!"

"And then that thing chased us all the way over here!" Shaggy cried.

"The frozen giant chased you?" Daphne asked. "Wait a minute. Where's Velma?"

Shaggy looked around, as if he'd just remembered that Velma was missing. "Like, that's what I want to know! The giant was hot on our heels when we bolted out of that cave. But all of a sudden, Velma wasn't."

"So Velma's missing?" Fred asked. "I have a feeling if we find Velma, we'll also find Sabrina."

Norah groaned. "So what you're saying is, you think the frozen giant has two prisoners now? But why?" She looked at the others and shook her head. "Maybe I should just cancel the Ice Carnival and close up town again. This is getting too dangerous!"

"Reah," Scooby said. "Rangerous!"

"Look over here!" Daphne exclaimed suddenly.

"It looks like that giant dropped something when it was chasing you," she said. She was holding a large piece of paper.

Shaggy shook his head. "The giant is a litterbug."

"Rad riant," Scooby said.

"This isn't litter," Daphne said, unfolding the paper. "It's another clue. This is a map!"

"Not just any map," Fred said. He looked over Daphne's shoulder. "It's a map of the forest and hills surrounding the town of Giant's Ridge."

"Why would the giant need a map of the forest?" Shaggy asked. "If it's really been hanging out in these hills for a thousand years, wouldn't it know its way around by now?"

Fred nodded. "You're exactly right, Shaggy. If the giant really had spent a lot of time around Giant's Ridge, it certainly wouldn't need a map." He folded the map and tucked it inside his pocket. "This is all starting to make a lot more sense. I have a hunch about who our frozen giant might be. We need to find Velma and Sabrina. Then it's time to set a trap!"

CHAPTER

8

Fred, Daphne, Norah, Shaggy, and Scooby-Doo followed their footprints back through the forest to the hidden caves. There was no sign of the frozen giant anywhere. But that didn't mean he wasn't hiding somewhere. Shaggy hoped the giant wouldn't pounce at them as they walked past.

As they neared the entrance to the cave, the gang could hear ice shattering and breaking inside. "Someone's in there," Fred said.

Shaggy and Scooby both stopped in their tracks. "Like, it sounds like the frozen giant to me! Run!" Shaggy cried.

"Reah, run!" Scooby barked.

That's when they heard Velma's voice calling to them. "Fred! Daphne! Shaggy! In here!"

They followed the sound of Velma's voice. As they waited for their eyes to adjust to the darkness inside the cave, they could hear the sounds of ice crystals crashing to the ground.

"Guys, we're over this way," Velma called.

Shaggy and Scooby peered through the darkness. They were looking for Velma, but they were also keeping their eyes open for any sign of the frozen giant.

"*Psst*, Shaggy! Scooby!" Velma cried. "You're looking right at me."

Scooby hid behind Shaggy as they stepped farther into the darkness. "Relma?" he asked. The only thing he could see was a pile of ice that looked like the wall of the cave. But as the two buddies inched closer, they could see it was some sort of icy cage. Velma and Sabrina were trapped inside!

Fred, Daphne, and Norah came rushing over. Together, they kicked at the ice, but it wouldn't budge or break enough for Velma and Sabrina to escape.

"We need something that will melt this ice," Fred said, scratching at his head.

"The only thing in this cave is a big bag of salt," Shaggy said, pointing. "Like, the frozen giant must like his soft pretzels extra salty or something." Shaggy's stomach growled. "Oh, man, I'm so hungry I'd trade my mittens for a soft pretzel right about now."

"Salt!" Velma cried. "Shaggy, salt will melt the

ice! Shake it on the walls of this ice cage. Then we can get out of here."

They all got to work pouring salt on the walls of the frozen cage.

"Hurry," Velma said. "The giant isn't here now, but I'm sure it'll be back soon."

As they worked, Daphne said, "The giant must have been throwing salt at all the ice houses when it crashed through town. It was trying to ruin the ice carvings by melting them!"

"I think you're right, Daphne," Fred said. "Now I *know* we're on the right track for solving this mystery. It's just a matter of getting the giant to come out so we can melt its plans and save the Ice Carnival!"

The salt had finally melted the frozen walls enough that Velma and Sabrina could climb out of their ice cage.

"Thank you," Sabrina gushed. "You saved me. I was afraid that frozen beast was going to keep me here forever."

"We heard you yelling for help," Fred said. "But when we went in the caves to look for you, it was quiet again."

"I *was* yelling for help. But just before Velma, Shaggy, and Scooby came into the cave, the giant gagged me," Sabrina said. "Luckily for me, the giant caught Velma and put her in here, too.

Otherwise, I would still be gagged. You would have never found me if it weren't for Velma! She untied me and saved us both."

"I'm just glad we're safe," Velma said. "Now it's time for us to give the giant a taste of his own medicine and trap him in his own icy cage. Let's get to work, gang!"

"First, we have to figure out a way to get the giant to come out of hiding again," Fred said. "If we can get it to follow us into town, we can trap it."

"Rap rit?" Scooby asked. He was munching on a piece of salty ice from the giant's cage.

Everyone was looking at him strangely. "Rhut? Rit's rummy."

Shaggy leaned over and took a lick. "You're right, Scoob. It *is* yummy. Like salty ice cream. But it would taste even better with a nice, hot cup of chili." His tummy grumbled, echoing through the cave. "Speaking of which . . . *I'm* getting pretty chilly in here."

"Scooby, Shaggy, if we can get the giant to follow us into town, we need you to run straight for the pirate ship," Fred instructed. He led the gang out of the cave and into the forest again.

Shaggy crunched on a piece of frozen ice. "Like, I hope you're gonna tell me there's a four-course meal set up in that ice boat. Because the only place I'm running is *away* from the giant and *toward* my next meal."

"Reah," Scooby agreed.

"Will you help us trap the giant if I give you a Scooby Snack?" Velma offered.

Scooby set down his ice. "Rooby rack?" He thought for a moment. "Ruh-uh."

"How about *two* Scooby Snacks?" Velma said.

"Rope," Scooby said, shaking his head.

Sabrina suddenly spoke up. "What if I promise to fill my ice castle with Scooby Snacks? You can eat them all."

Scooby jumped up and down. "Rokay!"

"Like, what's in it for me?" Shaggy asked.

"If we solve this mystery and make the giant go away, the Ice Carnival will be back on again," Daphne said.

Norah nodded. "And that means we'll have the ice-cream eating contest tomorrow. "

Shaggy and Scooby high-fived.

"I guess now we just need to get that giant to come out of hiding," Fred said, adjusting his scarf. He put his hand over his eyes and peered around the forest. "How on earth are we going to do that?"

"Guys?" Shaggy said. "Like, I think that's not going to be a problem. Look!"

Everyone turned. The frozen giant was charging through the forest. It was headed straight toward them.

"Ruh-roh," Scooby whimpered. "Ret's run."

"Like, again!" Shaggy cried. He waved his arms in the air and jogged around in circles.

"Follow me, everyone," Norah began to hustle through the woods the other way. "I know the way back to town."

Scooby's tongue was out and he panted as they flew through the forest. After a few moments, Norah and the gang could see the edge of town up ahead. They were almost there, but the giant was right on their heels and closing in fast.

"Are you ready to run for the pirate ship, guys?" Fred asked.

"As ready as I'll ever be," Shaggy answered.

The group ran down the town's main street. Shaggy and Scooby leaped through the door of the icy pirate ship. They jumped up onto the deck to put as much distance between them and the giant as possible. The giant was close enough that it could reach out one hand and touch them. It stormed into the pirate ship behind them.

Just then, Fred dropped the ship's fishing net straight onto the giant! It was trapped like a huge fish on a frozen sea. The beast thrashed inside the net.

The giant reached one hand through the net to grab Scooby's tail. Shaggy and Scooby slipped out of the boat through a porthole. The giant was still caught inside.

But as the two buddies ran for safety, the giant shook free of the net! Now it was really angry. It started after them.

Shaggy ran toward a snowplow that was parked at the edge of the town square. "Like, let's hide in here, Scooby!"

The giant was just a few steps behind them. That's when Scooby noticed the keys were in the snowplow. "Rook!"

"Not now, old pal," Shaggy said nervously.

"I don't think it's a good time for a joyride in a snowplow, if you know what I mean."

Scooby pointed at the giant, and then at the big shovel on the front of the snowplow. "Oh," Shaggy said, realizing what Scooby was trying to tell him. "Scoob, you're a genius! We can shovel up the giant!"

"Res!" Scooby cried.

Shaggy turned the snowplow on, and it roared toward the frozen giant. As they drove through the square, the plow's front shovel filled with snow. The giant realized what was happening a few seconds too late. The plow reached down and scooped the giant up.

A few seconds later, they dumped the beast into a pile of snow. The rest of the snow from the plow landed on top of the giant. The frozen giant was trapped in a mound of ice and snow!

Norah and the rest of the gang came running over with shovels. "Good thinking, guys!" Fred exclaimed. They all began digging the giant out of the snow pile.

As they uncovered the giant's head, Velma asked, "Are you ready to see who our frozen giant is?"

CHAPTER
10

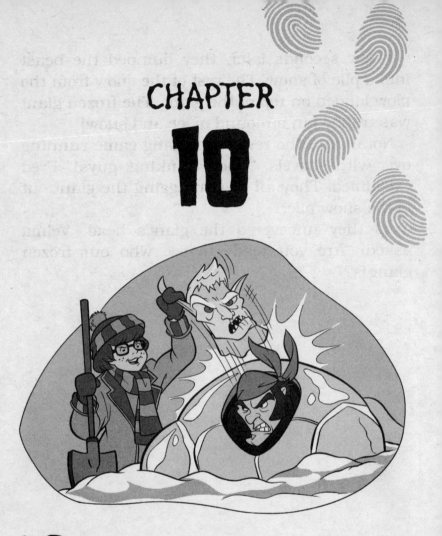

"**S**oren Gray!" Norah cried.

"Just as we suspected," Velma said.

"But I don't understand why one of the ice artists would try to ruin the Ice Carnival," Norah cried.

Soren Gray sat miserably in the pile of snow. His arms were still trapped inside the snow bank. "You tried to trap me inside my own ship," he muttered.

Norah was still shaking her head. "So . . . does this mean the frozen giant definitely isn't real? It was Soren Gray, dressed up in a costume all along?"

"It looks that way," Fred said. "Soren Gray was using the legend of the frozen giant to try to scare people out of Giant's Ridge."

"How on earth did you figure out it was just someone in costume?" Sabrina asked, staring at the other ice carver. "The giant seemed so real!"

"Reah," Scooby agreed, holding his tail. "Real."

Velma put one finger in the air. "We knew the giant was really just someone in a costume when we found our first big clue—the boot prints in the snow. A real giant wouldn't be wearing regular winter boots . . . it just doesn't make any sense."

Fred nodded. "As soon as we figured out that we were looking for a person, instead of a real giant, we began to hunt for clues."

"There were three obvious suspects," Daphne said. "It was just a matter of figuring out who our frozen giant really was."

"The first person that looked suspicious was Isabella Hooperman," Velma said. "She had plenty of reasons to scare people away from Giant's Ridge. But when we found traces of red glitter paint outside the caves in the forest, we realized our giant was either Lynn Johnson or Soren Gray."

Soren Gray grumbled from inside the snow bank.

"That's right," Fred agreed. "We saw Lynn Johnson spraying all the welcome signs with red painted *X*'s when we arrived this morning. She really wants people to leave Giant's Ridge. She's worried about tourists coming into town and pushing the bears and wolves out of the forest."

"But we're leaving the forest around our town alone!" Norah cried. "I would never do anything to hurt the forest or the animals' natural habitat. They're a big part of what makes Giant's Ridge so special!"

"You should probably talk to Lynn Johnson about that," Daphne suggested. "She's very worried."

Velma nodded. "The other person that we suspected was Soren Gray. When we were talking to him about his pirate ship ice carving, he told us he was planning to paint the ship a sparkling red."

"But how did you know who it really was?"

Norah asked. "It sounds like it really could have been either of them."

"I was sure that Soren was our giant when we found a map of the woods and caves," Fred said. "Lynn Johnson knows this area so well that she wouldn't need a map to find her way around. The giant was obviously someone who was unfamiliar with the forest and hills around Giant's Ridge."

"Also," Velma added, "every time we saw Lynn Johnson, she was wearing snowshoes. Not boots."

Daphne looked at Soren Gray. "And you're the only person who had a reason to melt the other ice houses and kidnap Sabrina," she added. "Sabrina's ice castle was the best ice carving in the whole competition. But if she didn't have time to finish, you would have a better chance of winning."

"I deserved to win!" Soren Gray spit out angrily. "I'm the best ice carver in the entire world. That prize money should be mine! I would have gotten away with this, if it weren't for you meddling kids and your wiggling dog."

"Well, you're certainly not going to win the competition now," Norah said. "You're going to jail—we need to get you out of here so the rest of us can enjoy the Ice Carnival!"

"And don't forget about the ice-cream eating contest!" Shaggy reminded them.

"Rand the Rooby Racks," Scooby said, bounding over to Sabrina's ice castle.

"A promise is a promise," Sabrina laughed.

Norah nodded. "And since Scooby is the one who figured out how to stop the giant once and for all, I guess we really owe you!"

"Rhat's right!" Scooby barked, and everyone laughed. "Scooby-Dooby-Doo!"